Dearie Deer

Written and illustrated by

Rita Kerr

EAKIN PRESS ★ Austin, Texas

This book is dedicated to

the author's many special friends,

including David and Bryan Toifl

and Larry Bowen.

FIRST EDITION

Copyright © 1998
By Rita Kerr

Published in the United States of America
by Eakin Press
A Division of Sunbelt Media, Inc.
P.O. Drawer 90159 ★ Austin, TX 78709
e-mail: eakinpub@sig.net

2   3   4   5   6   7   8   9

ISBN 1-57168-273-2

Library of Congress Cataloging-in-Publication Data

Kerr, Rita.
　　Dearie deer / written and illustrated by Rita Kerr.
　　　　p.　　cm.
　　Summary: A family raises and rehabilitates a fawn, whose mother has been killed by poachers, in order to return her to the wild.
　　ISBN 1-57168-273-2
　　1. White-tailed deer—Juvenile fiction. [1. White-tailed deer—Fiction. 2. Poaching—Fiction. 3. Wildlife rehabilitation—Fiction.] I. Title.
　　PZ10.3.K486D3   1998
　　[Fic]--dc21
　　　　　　　　　　　　　　　　　　　　　　　　　　　　　　98-35766
　　　　　　　　　　　　　　　　　　　　　　　　　　　　　　CIP
　　　　　　　　　　　　　　　　　　　　　　　　　　　　　　AC

Contents

There was a baby deer in the middle of the floor!

The Poacher

Davy and his father stopped abruptly at the kitchen door. They couldn't believe their eyes. There was a baby deer in the middle of the floor!

"Mary, where did that come from?" Davy's father asked his wife.

"Sammie found her in the woods behind the barn while you all were gone," she answered.

Sammie was the family dog. That collie was always finding stray animals.

Davy watched the fawn. It was not moving. "Is she dead?"

"Not yet," his mother said, "but if she doesn't get some milk she will be. That's why I brought her home with me." She turned to her husband. "George, do you think she'll have trouble taking this bottle?"

"She might," he replied. "Son, why don't you see if you can get her to suck on your finger while your mother is heating that milk?"

"Okay, I'll try." Davy tossed his books onto the table and sat down by the deer.

"Honey, did you see the fawn's mother?" George asked.

"Yes, she's dead. Someone shot her!" Mary said as she took a pan from the stove.

"But I put 'NO HUNTING' and 'KEEP OUT!' signs everywhere!"

"George, whoever shot that fawn's mother must have done it last night. Maybe he couldn't see the signs in the dark."

Sammie moved over close to Davy as he sat down on the floor. Davy rubbed the fawn's nose as he slowly eased his finger into her mouth. He giggled. "She is sucking on my finger and it tickles! Dad, I thought hunting season was over."

"It is," his father answered. "It ended the second week in January."

Davy's mother shook her head. "It was bad enough that the mother deer was shot, but that poacher left two babies to die."

"Poacher? What's a poacher?" Davy asked.

"A poacher is someone who hunts without permission," his father answered. "Mary, you say

2

there were two fawns?" He looked around the kitchen. "Where's the other one?"

"Dead, I'm sorry to say. About an hour ago I heard Sammie barking. I could tell something was wrong. He was making an awful racket. I went out to see what was the matter. Sammie found the mother near our back fence. The fawns were not far away hiding in the bushes. The other one was already dead."

Davy shook his head sadly.

Mary sighed as she slipped the nipple onto the bottle. "When a mother deer has a baby, she nudges the baby to its feet to get it to a safe hiding place. It stays perfectly still when the mother goes off to eat."

"Couldn't a coyote or some other wild animal get it?" Davy asked.

"Fawns have no odor. The mother stays nearby. Most deer spend their whole lives near the place where they were born. Now, let's see if we can get her to take this milk." Mary gathered the fawn into her arms as she sat down. "Come on, dearie, open your mouth. That's it."

"Dearie. That's a cute name. We can call her Dearie Deer!" Davy laughed as he reached for a paper towel. "It's running out the side of her mouth, she's so hungry!"

And she was.

"Son, run to the garage and get the white blanket from the shelf. She's shivering. While you are there, bring that empty box from the shelf. It will make a good bed for her."

Davy was back in no time.

"Now, help me wrap this blanket around her . . . There. She will be nice and warm. She was hungry. I put almost four ounces of milk in that bottle and she drank it all. If she lives, we'll need some more goat's milk and deer food from the feed store." Mary paused as she gazed at the fawn. "*Sh-h,* she's asleep."

Davy whispered, "Isn't she cute?"

"Yes, but if she lives, she will grow quickly."

"Mary, why don't we put her box over there in the corner so we can keep an eye on her?" George suggested.

"That's a good idea," she replied.

"Dad, can we keep her? Please? We could call her Dearie Deer," Davy begged.

"Son," George said as he sat down at the table, "I know you would like to keep her, but we can't."

Davy stared at his father. "But why not? She wouldn't eat very much."

His father sighed. "Everybody loves baby animals. There is nothing cuter than a tiger or lion

4

cub. But they do grow up. Would you want a grown tiger or lion for a pet? No, of course not. Well, fawns are cute but they grow up too. Deer belong in the woods."

"Shucks," Davy grumbled unhappily.

"That is not the only reason we should not keep her. Did you know that it is against the law to keep most wild animals? You need a special permit to raise them."

Davy was surprised. "Against the law? Why?"

"When people take them in and feed them, the animals get used to people," his father explained. "We say they get imprinted to humans."

"And what's wrong with that?" Davy demanded.

"Well, when they grow up, they are not afraid of people. That makes those animals easy targets for hunters," his father said.

"And poachers!" Davy cried.

"That's right," Mary said. "George, there are some tire tracks in the soft mud near the fence where Sammie found the deer. Whoever shot that doe knocked down a couple of our fenceposts. That poacher probably wanted to blind her with his headlights. The doe never had a chance."

Davy clinched his teeth. "Oh-h, I hope they get the guy!"

"Whoever shot that doe knocked down a couple of our fenceposts," Davy's mother said.

"I think I'll call the sheriff," Mary decided. "He might be interested in our poacher and those tire tracks."

"That's a good idea," George said as she reached for the telephone.

"Hello, this is Mary Rees. May I speak to the sheriff?" She paused to listen. "Really? That's awful." She paused again. "Yes, will you have him call me when he comes in? We had a poacher last night and I think he might be interested in the tire tracks that were left by our fence. Thank you."

"What did they say?" George asked as she hung up the phone.

"Sheriff Jones went out to the wildlife park with the game warden. It seems someone shot one of the big buffaloes at the park last night."

"But why would anyone shoot a buffalo?" Davy cried. He knew the park was special. People from all over Texas came to Kerrville to drive through the park and take pictures. There were hundreds of unusual animals from all over the world there. Davy doubled up his fist. "I hope the warden gets the guy!"

"Son," Davy's father said, "if your mother doesn't need you, we'd better go fix that fence. We don't want the cows getting out. We'll take the

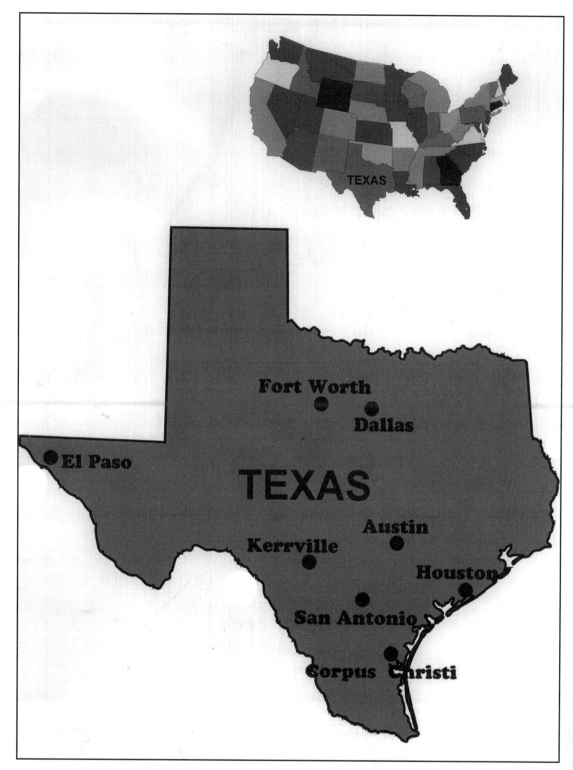

People from all over Texas came to Kerrville to visit the wildlife park.

shovel along so we can bury that dead fawn and her mother after the sheriff looks at them."

"Run along, Davy, and help your father. I will feed the chickens," Mary said.

"Gee, thanks. I'm ready when you are, Dad."

"George," Mary said, "when Sheriff Jones calls back, I will tell him about our poacher and the tire tracks. What should I tell him if he wants to come out and talk to you?"

"Just tell him to drive down the back road. That way he can't miss us," George answered as he and Davy headed for the door with Sammie at their heels.

The Tire Tracks

Davy helped his father gather the tools. "Do we have everything?" he asked.

"We've got the fenceposts, the nails, the shovel, the hoe, the hammer. I think that's everything. You and Sammie hop into the truck. Let's go."

They circled around behind the barn and drove across the field. Just past the trees they came to a stop near the fence.

When they got out of the truck, Davy and his father walked over to look at the tracks. "Your mother's right," George said. "The sheriff might find those tracks interesting. Come on. Let's get busy."

"Shucks," Davy muttered, "they just look like plain old car tracks in the mud to me."

A truck marked PARKS AND WILDLIFE *drove up.*

11

They had just hammered the last nail in the fencepost when a truck marked PARKS AND WILDLIFE drove up. Two men got out and walked toward them.

"Hello, Warden. Good to see you, Sheriff," Davy's father called.

"Howdy, George," Sheriff Jones said. He smiled down at Davy. "Boy, you're growing like a weed. You'll catch up with me before long."

Davy smiled. "I hope so." Sheriff Jones was over six feet tall.

"George, I understand you had a poacher and he left some tire tracks," the sheriff said.

"That's right. Come take a look at them."

The men squatted down to study the tracks more closely. When they stood up, the sheriff said, "Very interesting. From the looks of the tread on that right tire, it was old and worn thin. The left one looks like it was brand new. I'll get my camera and take some pictures. We might need them later. George, your wife said something about your poacher killing a deer and hitting your fence. Is that right?"

"Yes, and we had to put up a couple of new posts. The two he knocked down are over there," Davy's father replied.

"Warden, why don't you and George look

around for other clues while I take these pictures?" the sheriff said.

Davy and his dog were eager to help. Davy was the first to see the red marks on one of the old fenceposts. "Look! What's this?" he cried.

"Hmm-m, looks like paint from a car or truck," the game warden said. "If it is paint, we might be able to tell what kind of automobile it was. Look, there's some more on this post. George, is it all right if we take these posts back with us?"

"Sure, we don't need them."

The warden walked over and stared down at the dead doe. "He shot her twice."

Davy spoke up. "Yes, and one of her babies is over there in the bushes. Dad and I are going to dig a hole and bury them."

"I'll get the shovels out of the truck and we'll give you a hand," the warden said.

Sheriff Jones took out his knife. "Before we bury them, I want to get out those bullets to send to the lab. The lab can tell us what kind of gun that poacher used. Most of the time poachers use a .22. It doesn't make much noise."

"I'll get that fawn and we can bury them right here," George said. A few minutes later he yelled, "Son, run get that can of spray out of the truck.

"Sheriff, is it true that we need a permit to raise a baby deer?" Davy asked.

There are fire ants all over this fawn. That's probably what killed it."

While his father was spraying the ants, Davy looked up at the sheriff with his big blue eyes. "Sheriff, is it true that we need a permit to raise a baby deer?"

Sheriff Jones nodded. "It is true. We must protect the white-tailed deer and other wildlife. Many kinds of animals are already extinct."

"Extinct? What's that mean?"

"It means that there are none of that kind of animal left on the earth." The sheriff went on. "That's why we have laws to protect our wildlife. Deer belong in the wild, not around people."

Davy tried again. "But if I found a baby animal all alone, couldn't I keep it?"

Mr. Jones shook his head. "If you find a wild animal, you should call the game warden. He would tell you what to do."

"Well, Mr. Game Warden, we don't need to call." Davy's father laughed. "We've got a fawn in our kitchen. Thank goodness Mary took it up to the house before the fire ants got it too. What do you want us to do with it?"

"I'll have to check," the warden replied. "It takes special training to know how to care for wild animals. People with that special training work in what we call rehabilitation centers."

"Re-ha-bil-i-ta-tion," Davy muttered softly. "That's a funny word."

The game warden smiled. "We rehabilitate birds and mammals so they can be put back into the wild. We have several of those centers in this area, but this time of year they are usually pretty busy. I will have to call you, George."

"But why can't we keep her?" Davy asked.

The warden smiled down at him. "You don't have a permit to rehabilitate wild animals. That is why."

"Where can I get one?" Davy demanded.

"People who have had special training in caring for wild animals and birds get their permits from the state government in Austin," the warden said. He looked at the sheriff. "Well, that's all we can do here."

Sheriff Jones rubbed his chin as he said, "Now, let's look at our clues. We know that a red truck or car with a new left front tire and an old right one hit those fenceposts hard enough to chip the paint. That's a start. Warden, give me a hand and we'll put that fencepost in the truck. I think we'll drive back by the wildlife park and look for tire tracks before it gets dark. I've got a feeling that when we find the poacher who shot this deer, we'll find the guy who did the shooting at the park.

George, if you should find any more clues, let us know."

"We will," Davy called as the men got into their truck.

As they drove away, his father said, "Come on, son. Let's gather up our tools and head home."

That night they talked about the tire tracks and the red paint while they were eating. After Dearie had her bottle, Davy sat in the corner and drew pictures of her. Dearie watched him with her big brown eyes.

"I'm not going to hurt you," Davy whispered as he patted her head. "I'm your friend. So is Sammie."

Sammie wagged his tail excitedly. Dearie did not move as the dog licked her soft round nose with his long pink tongue. The white spots on her little tummy went up and down as she breathed. Davy tried not to think about giving her up and never seeing her again.

When it was time for bed, Davy looked at his mother. "Mama, Dearie's had her bottle. Can she sleep in my room?"

His mother shook her head. "No, Davy."

"But . . ."

"No buts about it," Davy's father said, glancing up from his paper.

Davy sat in the corner and drew pictures of Dearie.

"But . . ."

"No buts about it, David Bryan. You can't sleep with that deer, and that's final."

When his father called him David Bryan, Davy knew he had better not say any more. Not for a while, anyway.

Davy's Pet

Davy yawned and stretched as he sat up in bed the next morning. Then he remembered Dearie. He hopped out of bed and ran to the kitchen. His mother was giving Dearie her bottle. "Good morning, Mama. How is she?"

Mary smiled. "She's much better. I think she is going to live, but we must keep that door closed so she'll stay in here. She was out of her box a few minutes ago. We'll move her out on the screen porch this afternoon when you get home from school."

"Do I have to go to school? Can't I stay home and play with Dearie?"

His mother shook her head. "This is the last day of school. You will have the whole summer to play. Run along now and get ready for school. Your father doesn't like to wait." Davy always rode with his father. He passed by Davy's school on his way to work. He taught science at the local college.

As soon as Davy got to his class, the teacher walked in. "Good morning, children," she said.

"Good morning, teacher," they answered.

"Students," the teacher said, looking around the room, "does anyone have something interesting to tell us?"

Davy raised his hand.

"Yes, Davy," the teacher said.

"I've got a new pet!"

Billy spoke out. "What kind of pet?"

"I've got a baby deer! I call her Dearie Deer!"

"A baby deer? Where did you get her?" the teacher asked.

The children listened as Davy told his story. He told them that it was against the law to keep a baby white-tailed deer. They asked him all sorts of questions. Davy felt very important.

"Class," the teacher said, "would you like to write a story about what you will do this summer?"

"Oh, yes," they cried.

Davy wrote his story about Dearie. This is his story:

MY DEARIE

I have a baby deer. She is brown with white spots on her sides. My mother says that the spots will go away when she is older. My deer drinks milk from a bottle. She sleeps in a box in our kitchen. I call her Dearie Deer. My dog Sammie found her. Some guy shot Dearie's mother and a buffalo at the park. I hope they catch him. I wish I could keep Dearie, but I can't. It's against the law. The game warden is trying to find Dearie a home where she will be safe from hunters.

After lunch the children played games and had a party. All of the time Davy kept worrying about Dearie. What if the game warden came and took her away before he got home?

Caught!

After school Davy raced through the living room with Sammie at his heels. "Mama, can Dearie go out on the porch with us?"

His mother laughed. "You mean can you go on the porch with Dearie? She has been there most of the afternoon. It is so nice and warm. I moved her box out in the sunshine. Before long she can go out in the yard with you. Why don't you see if she will play ball with you?"

The deer was not sure she wanted to play ball at first. Sammie wanted to play. When they rolled the ball between her legs, Dearie leaped into the air and ran to the other end of the porch. She watched Sammie and Davy roll the ball back and forth to each other. It was not long before Dearie was rolling the ball to them with her nose.

*It was not long before Dearie was rolling
the ball to them with her nose.*

When it was time for Davy to feed the chickens, Dearie wanted to go. "No, you stay here," Davy said as he and Sammie headed for the door. Dearie pressed her nose against the screen wire as she watched them walk toward the barn.

Each time the telephone rang, Davy crossed his fingers and held his breath. He was afraid that it might be the game warden. Davy never knew that time could pass so quickly. When he wasn't busy helping his mother, Davy played with Dearie.

"Mama," he said, "I think her spots are bigger!"

His mother laughed. "That's because her tummy is getting fatter."

On Saturday, Davy held Dearie in his arms and fed her a bottle of milk. Dearie felt so soft and cuddly. He hated to put her back into her box.

That afternoon they took Dearie outside in the warm sunshine. Her big ears stood straight up as she tagged along after Sammie. She looked like a puppy. It was fun watching Dearie's short brown and white tail flop up and down as she jumped through the grass on her long skinny legs. Davy never knew a fawn's legs could be so long!

"Dearie, you're all legs!" Davy cried. He had an idea when he saw his red wagon. "Would you like a ride?" he asked as he put her into the wagon.

That afternoon they took Dearie out into the sunshine.

Dearie sat down with a *thud* when the wagon began moving. Her eyes were as big as saucers! She shook with fear. "Aw, Dearie, I didn't mean to scare you," Davy said as he rubbed her nose. "That wasn't so bad was it? You can run play with Sammie."

The next thing Davy knew, the deer jumped back into the wagon and sat down. Davy laughed. "All right, I will pull you some more." Sammie ran along beside the wagon barking.

Davy had an idea. He got an old rope from the porch and looped it through the handle of the wagon then through the dog's collar. "Come on, Sammie. You pull her," he said. Sammie started off across the yard with the wagon trailing along behind him. Davy laughed and laughed. His mother watched them from the porch. She was not sure who was having the most fun—Davy or Sammie or Dearie. She got her camera and took some pictures of the three of them.

By evening, they were all tired. Dearie was ready for her supper. So were Davy and Sammie.

The next morning Dearie was finishing her bottle when Davy ran into the kitchen.

"Good morning, Davy," his mother said.

"Good morning, Mama. How's Dearie?"

"Full and sleepy!" His mother whispered as

"Come on, Sammie. You pull her," Davy cried.

she put the deer into her box. "Son, we don't want to be late for church. You and your father can have toast and cereal for breakfast. You all can eat while I'm getting ready. I think I'll wear my new dress."

"Okay, Mama, I'll fix the toast." Davy had everything on the table when his father came in. Then his mother appeared at the door in her new dress.

"How pretty you look!" Davy said.

"Thank you, and how handsome you look," she said as she looked them over. "I guess we are ready. Davy, maybe you'd better put Sammie outside. And I'll close this door. I don't want Dearie going into the living room."

"It feels like summer is here," Davy's father remarked as they backed out of the driveway. He was right. There were many bright colored flowers beside the road—yellow daisies and cornflowers and buttercups.

Davy could hardly wait to tell his friends about Dearie. When they got to church, everyone was talking about how the sheriff had caught the poacher who had shot the animals at the wildlife park.

Davy heard someone say, "Did you hear the news? They caught that poacher!"

Another said, "I'm glad they caught that guy

"A deer for a dear," the pastor said.

before he shot any more animals. He had been in lots of trouble before. What kind of a fellow would shoot a buffalo anyway? Buffalo are almost extinct. We've got to protect them."

Everyone was so busy talking about the poacher, they did not have time to listen to Davy. But he told everyone who would listen about his baby deer. When he told the pastor, the pastor smiled and patted him on the head and said, "That is nice, Davy. A deer for a dear!"

Everyone laughed. Davy did not see what was so funny.

The Mess

Davy was out of the car as soon as they stopped in the driveway. He wanted to see Dearie. She was waiting for them when they unlocked the door.

"Hey, how . . ." Davy did not finish. The living room was a mess! One of the chairs had been turned over. The end table by the sofa was upside down. There were papers and magazines all over the floor.

"Oh, my!" his mother cried. "I know I shut that kitchen door! Dearie must have pushed it open."

Davy tried to catch Dearie before she jumped over the sofa and raced down the hall. "I'll get her," he cried as he took off after her. Sammie was right behind him, barking all the way. The deer ran into Davy's room and leaped up on the bed.

"I'll get her," Davy cried as he took off after Dearie.

"Come on, Dearie, you've got to go back to the kitchen," Davy yelled.

The deer had other ideas. She leaped across the bed, out the door, and down the hall before Davy could catch her. Davy and Sammie had a wild chase through the other bedrooms. They finally trapped Dearie in the bathroom.

"Don't worry, Mama, we got her. She's in your bathtub!"

"Oh, my. I do hope she doesn't chip the paint in my tub with her sharp hoofs. Just look at my lamp and my vase—the one my mother gave me." There were pieces of glass everywhere.

"I'll clean it up," Davy cried. He headed for the kitchen to get the broom.

"Don't cry, honey," Davy's father said, patting Mary on the arm. "We'll get you another lamp. You run along and change your clothes. Davy and I will clean up this mess."

Davy was worried about Dearie. From the look on his father's face, Davy knew he was not happy. What was going to happen to Dearie?

When everything was back in place, they put Dearie out on the screened porch. No one said much while they were eating.

"Davy," his mother said when they had

finished, "you know we must do something about Dearie, don't you?"

"Yes, Mama. But . . . I love her!" Davy stared down at his plate. A tear rolled slowly down his cheek.

"I know, son. It is because you love Dearie that you must let her go." His father patted his hand. "The longer we keep her, the harder it will be to let her go. In the excitement of catching that poacher, maybe the warden forgot all about her. I'll call him and see where he wants us to take her."

Just then the phone rang.

"I will answer it," Davy's father said as he reached for the phone. "Hello . . . I was just going to call you, Warden . . . Yes, we will be home. That's fine. We will see you when you get here. Good-bye."

Davy fought back the tears.

"Well, that's settled," his father said as he looked across the table.

"Where's he taking her? Can we go see her?"

George shook his head. "No, Davy. We must forget about Dearie and she must forget about us. It will be hard for you but it will be hard for her too. Even in this short time, Dearie has become imprinted to the sound of our voices, the kitchen,

"You know we must do something about Dearie,"
Davy's mother said.

Sammie, everything. She must forget about us so she can grow up and live in the wild."

Davy wiped his sleeve across his nose. "I'll try."

His mother smiled. "Son, we know it will not be easy for you to let her go, but you must. Just remember, Dearie will be with other deer where she will be safe."

They heard Sammie barking before they heard the car. "That must be the warden," George said as he headed for the door. "Come on in. Good to see you. Would you like a cup of coffee and something to eat?"

The warden shook his head. "No, thanks. I can't stay. Sorry I've been so slow getting back to you. This has been some week! Wish I had time to sit down and visit, but I still have work to do. I brought a cage along. So, I'll just get that fawn and run along."

"Where are you taking her?" Davy cried. "Can't we just drive by and see her?"

The man shook his head. "No, boy. It is better this way. Think of it like this: You have had your very own deer for a little while. Now, every time you see a beautiful fawn, you can think of her. She's going to a place where she will grow up wild and free. That is the way it was meant to be."

"Come on, Davy. Tell Dearie good-bye. The warden is in a hurry," Mary said.

Davy ran to the porch and threw his arms around Dearie's neck. "Good-bye, Dearie Deer. You've got to forget about me and I've got to forget about you. Mama says it's because I love you that I must let you go. But I will always love you. I will never forget you. Good-bye."

"Come on, Dearie," George said as he gathered the fawn up into his arms. "You stay in the house, Davy."

Davy and Sammie ran to the window to watch as they put Dearie into the cage in the back of the truck. He did not see the two men shaking hands. He was crying too hard.

As the truck drove away, Davy threw his arms around his dog. Sammie licked his face.

"Dearie's gone, Sammie. We must forget about her," Davy said. Then he added, "But Sammie, if you find another wild animal, do me a favor. Please find one that we can keep."

"*Because I love you, I must let you go,*" Davy cried.

Wild and Free

Dearie was taken to a farm down a quiet country road. She was put into a stall with two other young deer. They sniffed at Dearie and she sniffed at them. She did not like the way they smelled. They did not smell like Davy.

Dearie did not like the stall, but she could not get out. There were strange round holes in one wall. She missed her box and Davy and Sammie. To make matters worse, she was hungry and thirsty.

She watched the other fawns eating some deer food off of the floor. She tried the food, but she did not like it. She tried the water in the bucket, but she did not like that either. She wanted her bottle.

Dearie was ready to give up in despair when she heard a noise. The other two deer ran to the strange holes in the wall when three nipples appeared. Dearie decided that getting milk from a bottle in a wall was better than nothing.

When her milk was gone, Dearie lay down in the corner but she could not sleep. It was so dark and still. She wondered where Davy was.

The next day came and went. So did the next and the next. The memory of the past slowly faded. Dearie thought less and less about Davy and Sammie and her box.

One day the big door to the stall was opened. The other deer ran out into the sunshine. Dearie was right behind them. In a nearby field she saw deer of all sizes. Some were eating. Others were running and jumping. It was almost dark when Dearie and the others were taken back to their stall.

After that, Dearie's days were much alike. She ate and slept and ran and played with the other deer. All the time she was growing and changing. Her spots were slowly fading away. She was wild and free!

One day Dearie was by the high fence near the road when she heard a truck. When the truck was near the fence a big dog suddenly stuck his head out of the window and started barking. Dearie lifted her head and stared at the dog. She watched

Dearie stared at the dog in the truck.

the truck as it moved off down the road. When it was gone, she kicked up her heels and ran off across the field.

"Dad, let's go back, let's go back! That was Dearie! I know it was!" Davy cried. "Did you see how she looked at Sammie and how he looked at her? Did you hear him barking? He never barks at deer. He knew it was Dearie! Please, Dad, can't we go back?"

Davy's father shook his head and kept on going. "She's gone now. She ran off. Besides, Davy, by now Dearie has forgotten about us. She is wild and free. That is the way it has to be."

Davy sat there for the longest time, then he threw his arms around Sammie's neck. "I guess Dad is right. Because we love Dearie, we must let her go. I guess that is the way it has to be."

Glossary

buck: male deer.
doe: female deer.
exotic: from another part of the world.
extinct: no longer living.
fawn: baby deer.
illegal: against the law.
imprinted: behavior learned early in life.
poacher: one who trespasses on another's land to take game or fish illegally.
rehabilitate: restore.
rehabilitator: one who restores.
wildlife: wild animals and plants.

Bibliography

Holloway, Cile. "House Panel to Eye Wild-animal Bill." *San Antonio Express-News*, April 2, 1997.

Watkins, Clara. *Kerr County Texas, 1856-1976*. Kerrville: Hill Country Preservation Society, Inc., 1982.

Williams, Lew. *A Pictorial History of Kerr County*. Missouri: D-Books Publishing, Inc., 1994.

Miscellaneous from Texas Parks and Wildlife Department

Armstrong, W. E. "Managing Habitat for White-tailed Deer in the Hill Country Area of Texas." Texas Parks and Wildlife Department, 1991.

Kerr Wildlife Management Area Driving Tour.

"Learn About Whitetails." *Texas Parks and Wildlife Magazine*, October 1992.

Parks and Wildlife Proclamations, Issued Under Authority of Texas Parks and Wildlife Code.

Perkins, J. R. "Supplemental Feeding." Texas Parks and Wildlife Department, 1991.

Texas Parks and Wildlife laws, State of Texas, 1995-1996. St. Paul: West Publishing Co.

Thomas, Jack. "Quantity vs. Quality." *Texas Parks and Wildlife Magazine*, October 1965.

Wildlife Parks of Texas

Bayou Wildlife Park at Alvin in Brazoria County. Eighty-six-acre habitat with a variety of exotic animals (281-337-6376).

Exotic Cat Refuge and Wildlife Orphanage at Kirbyville in Jasper County. Licensed orphanage for exotic cats and wildlife (409-423-4847).

Exotic Resort Zoo at Johnson City in Blanco County. Guided tours, petting area (210-868-4357).

Fossil Rim Wildlife Ranch at Glen Rose in Somervell County. Some thirty species of endangered animals roam 2,900 acres (817-897-2960).

Herring's Wildlife Park at Jacksonville in Cherokee County. Drive-through or guided tours (903-683-5358).

Kerrville Camera Safari at Kerrville in Kerr County. Hundreds of exotic animals from all over the world (210-792-3600).

Natural Bridge Wildlife Ranch near New Braunfels in Comal County. Exotic animals, birds, and Texas wildlife roam freely over 200 acres (210-651-6101).

Noah's Land Wildlife Park at Gonzales in Gonzales County. Drive through 400 acres where 110 species of exotic animals roam free. Petting compound (210-540-4654).

Topsey Exotic Ranch at Copperas Cove in Coryell County. Seventy species of animals, petting zoo for children (817-547-3700).

For additional information contact:

Texas Department of Transportation
1101 East Anderson Lane
Austin, Texas 78752

Acknowledgments

The author is grateful to librarians Betty Harborth, Dottie Kowalik, and Carol McClintock for their assistance in writing *Dearie Deer*. Thanks to Pam G. Toifl and her boys for their interest in this story. Special thanks to wildlife rehabilitators Shirley Ratisseau and Chris O'Quinn for sharing their expertise about rehabilitating animals to return them to the wild. Thanks goes to Kevin O'Neal at the Kerr Wildlife Management Office and to Game Warden Hilda Sanchez, Susette Dusterhft, and others of the Texas Parks and Wildlife Department for their help.

The author became interested in writing this story about protecting our wildlife when five different people in five different locations told of finding a baby deer and trying to raise it in their homes. The story took a different twist and had to be rewritten when the author learned that it is illegal to raise wildlife without a special permit. It is the author's hope that readers of *Dearie Deer* will become more aware of the importance of wildlife protection.

Other books by Rita Kerr:

The Alamo Cat
Buttercup and Bully Goat
Christopher and Pony Boy
Ghost of Panna Maria
Girl of the Alamo
Gray Eagle
The Haunted House
The Immortal 32
Juan Seguin
The Texas Cowboy
Texas Footprints
Texas Forever
Texas Marvel
The Texas Orphans
Texas Rebel
Texas Rose: The Story of Dilue Rose Harris
Tex's Tales
A Wee Bit of Texas

All available from
EAKIN PRESS, P.O. Drawer 90159, Austin, Texas 78709-0159
(1-800-880-8642 or eakinpub@sig.net).
The author presents an excellent educational program for schools and other
groups. Contact Rita Kerr at 210-826-4996.